MEET GORGON

MEET GORGON

Based on the television
episode **Meet Gorgon,** written by
Bill Braunstein

Adapted by Gerry Bailey

Illustrations by Henryk Szor

SCHOLASTIC INC.

New York   Toronto   London   Auckland   Sydney
Mexico City   New Delhi   Hong Kong   Buenos Aires

ISBN 0-439-37024-8

Published by Scholastic Inc. SCHOLASTIC and
associated logos are trademarks and/or registered
trademarks of Scholastic Inc.

12 11 10 9 8 7 6 5 4 3 2 1   1 2 3 4 5 6/0

Printed in the U.S.A.
First Scholastic printing, December 2001

MEET GORGON

THE BUTT-UGLY MARTIANS' THEME SONG

BKM! BKM! BKM! (ah ha!) BKM!
We are the Martians,
The Butt-Ugly Martians.
We are the Martians,
The Butt-Ugly Martians.

We don't really want a war.
I just want to hoverboard.
We don't want to conquer Earth.
I just want to fill my girth.

We are the Martians,
The Butt-Ugly Martians.
We are the Martians,
The Butt-Ugly Martians.

If you try to go too far,
You will see how tough we are.
If you try it any way,
Then you're gonna hear me say.

BKM! (oh yeah!) BBKM! (Let's get ugly!)
BKM! BBKM!
We are the Martians,
The Butt-Ugly Martians.
We are the Martians,
The Butt-Ugly Martians.

THE STORY SO FAR...

THE YEAR IS 2053 and the Martians
have landed on Earth! The advance troops
— Commander B.Bop-A-Luna,
Tech Commando 2-T-Fru-T and Corporal
Do-Wah Diddy — have been sent to Earth
by their ruthless leader, Emperor Bog,
to take over the planet.

Back on board the *Bogstar* spaceship,
Emperor Bog, along with his sidekick,
the evil Dr. Damage, is waiting for his
advance troops to complete the first
phase of the invasion. But the three Butt-
Ugly Martians love Earth so much, they
have no intention of taking it over!

Instead, they hang out with their
Earthling friends, Mike, Angela, and
Cedric, watching TV, eating fast food,

avoiding Stoat Muldoon — Earth's
number one Alien Hunter (or so he thinks!)
and generally enjoying themselves.

To convince Emperor Bog that the
invasion is progressing well, they
regularly send him fake battle reports.
Meanwhile, with the help of their
incredibly useful robotic canine, Dog, the
Butt-Uglies are actually Earth's heroes,
protecting the planet from alien attack!

B! K! M!

Sent to conquer planet Earth,
Our mission is now to protect it.
Courage to fight for freedom.
Wisdom to use these powers for
the good of mankind.
Power to defend against all invaders.

DAMAGE'S DIABOLICAL DEVICE

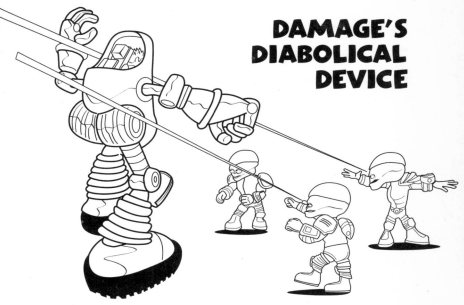

ON THE GROUND a fierce battle raged between the three Butt-Ugly Martians and a huge, powerful Exo-Bot. 2-T, Do-Wah, and B.Bop rapidly fired photon beams from their wrist gauntlets. But the Exo-Bot swung its clawed arms and deflected the beams into outer space.

Things were looking bad for the Martians. Then the mechanical monster turned round to reveal Mike, the Martian's best Earthling friend, at the controls! What kind of battle was this?

"Take this, you unwholesome Earth creature!" yelled B.Bop.

"Our laser beams don't seem to be having any effect," said 2-T.

"It's deflecting our photon beams!" yelled Do-Wah, acting as if death was staring him in the face.

"There must be a way to defeat this human," said 2-T, looking as serious as he could.

2

"I've got an idea. Cover me!" cried B.Bop as he made a run for it.

Do-Wah and 2-T nodded and began to fire even harder. As they advanced, they passed Dog, the Butt-Uglies' robo pooch, who was in broadcast mode, his eyes wide and glowing, as he recorded the action. This was no real battle. It was a fake report that was being recorded by Dog and beamed directly to the Martian Emperor, Bog, aboard his battle cruiser, the *Bogstar*.

Meanwhile, Mike's friends, Cedric and Angela, stood behind some rocks nearby. They were using a device created by

2-T, the Martian Tech Commando. The device was called an Invasion Battle Enhancer, and it made the battle seem even more real. Cedric pressed a button on the device and sent billows of smoke toward the battle. Angela pressed buttons on the other side of the keypad to make booms, bangs, and any other battle sounds she wanted.

"2-T's Exo-Bot is great, and this Battle Blaster works like a charm!" shouted Cedric as Angela hit another button. "Hey, what the...?" continued Cedric, as a sheeplike *baa* came from the machine.

"Sorry!" said Angela. "Wrong button."

The battle continued, but the Butt-Uglies were getting nowhere. Then B.Bop

reappeared aboard his One Martian Air Bike. He guided the OMAB over the Exo-Bot and began circling faster and faster. In no time, he had created a mini-tornado with the Exo-Bot in its eye.

The Exo-Bot began to spin around. Mike struggled with the controls, but he couldn't stop the machine from spinning. He began to look decidedly unwell!

"I think I'm going to..." he began. But before Mike could finish, the Exo-Bot had crashed to the ground.

2-T and Do-Wah danced a short victory dance right in front of Dog, who was still transmitting.

When Angela and Cedric reached Mike, he was not looking good.

"You okay?" Angela asked.

Cedric held up two fingers. "How many fingers am I holding up?" he asked.

"Thursday," replied Mike.

"He's okay." Cedric smiled.

Meanwhile, on the bridge of the mighty *Bogstar*, Emperor Bog and his sinister right-hand Martian, Dr. Damage, were watching the battle on the ship's screen.

"Well done, Martians," trumpeted Bog, as the triumphant Butt-Uglies completed their victory dance.

"As you can see, your Royal Highness," said B.Bop hurriedly, "the invasion of Earth continues to go well. So you have yourself a good day..."

Bog looked stern. "Not so fast. As a token of my appreciation, I believe a reward for this victory is appropriate. Damage, show our three advance troops your latest creation."

"Oh, don't you just love gifts." Do-Wah sighed.

Damage then revealed what looked like a squashed turtle with a handle and buttons.

7

"I have created the ultimate weapon," said Damage with pride. "A Molecular De-Atomizer..."

Meanwhile, at an unused military airfield back on Earth, someone was hacking into Bog's transmission. But that someone was no human. Leaning over and adjusting the focus on his Transmission Interceptor was the shape-shifting, technology-stealing alien known as Gorgon.

"Oh, hellooo..." he cooed.

Gorgon watched and grinned as the face of Dr. Damage appeared on his monitor. "And what do we have here?"

10

said the scaly alien, settling back to listen. "A transmission from the Martian fleet. Let's see what they're up to..."

"...Possibly the most powerful device I've ever created. It's sleek, compact, and will soon come in four designer colors," continued Damage.

"Get on with it, Damage!" shouted Emperor Bog impatiently.

Damage looked around. He whistled for one of Bog's Martian guards to step a little closer. The guard looked at the Molecular De-Atomizer and began to feel queasy. He closed his eyes in anticipation of a messy death.

"I just love this part." Bog laughed, swinging round in his chair and looking joyfully at Damage and the Martian guard.

Damage activated the Molecular De-Atomizer and a colorful orange-red bubble floated out of it and toward the shaking minion. But instead of striking the guard, it hit the laser staff he was holding in his hands. The bubble engulfed the weapon and with a muted crackle and pop, the laser staff disappeared! The guard opened his eyes and checked himself all over to make sure he was still in one minion piece.

The Butt-Ugly Martians were glued to their screen. "Very impressive, Damage," said B.Bop.

"Do you think that thing could remove toe fungus?" interrupted Do-Wah. "It's just that I've got this..."

2-T shoved an elbow into Do-Wah's side before he could finish.

Bog continued, "Damage will teleport the device to you. Whatever you do, don't let it fall into the wrong hands."

"We'll be standing by," said 2-T.

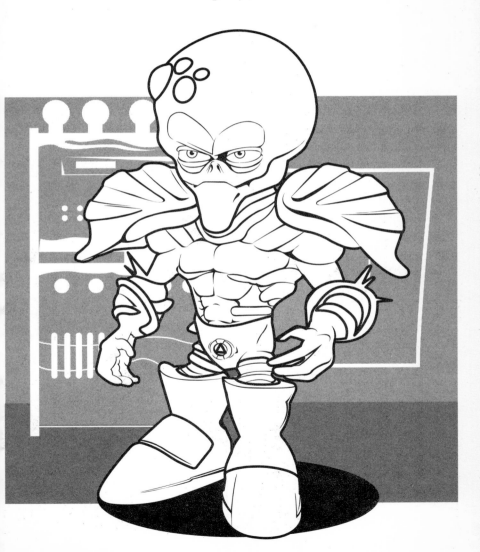

"Good," replied Bog. "Soon, Earth will be mine!" The Emperor of Mars pressed a button on the arm of his commander's chair and the transmission faded.

In his airfield lair, Gorgon smiled and muttered to himself, "Your plan might not be quite as straightforward as you think, Emperor Bog. Not if I get to Damage's device first!" He continued to smile as his eyes glowed fiery red.

GORGON STRIKES AGAIN

LATER THAT DAY, Cedric and Angela watched closely as Mike maneuvered the controls of the 1999 arcade game, Doomrace 2000. It was Mike's favorite old game in ZAPZ, the abandoned amusement arcade that was the Butt-Ugly Martians' hideout on Earth.

"Wooooh, 2-T, super job rebuilding Doomrace 2000," said Angela. "I bet it didn't work this well when it was new."

"Thanks, Angie," said 2-T. "I knew you guys would like it."

Cedric was thinking hard. "Do you have any idea what a retro game like this goes for? I heard about this collector guy. He paid two point three million bucks for a Donkey Kong arcade game — and it didn't even work!"

"He can't sell it," said Mike, trying to concentrate on the game. "It's loaded with Martian parts... Besides, I'm just about to set the record...oh, noooo!" The game finished suddenly, and Mike had just missed setting the all-time record, leaving him majorly disappointed.

Do-Wah decided to try and cheer him up. He came over to the teenagers with an open can in his hand. "Treat?" he asked.

Angela looked at the can. It was filled

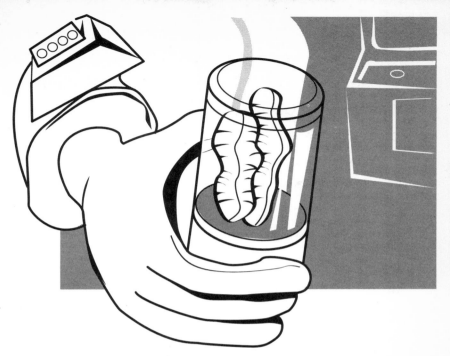

with slimy, gooey, crawly wormlike things. She drew away in horror. "Ugh! What are those things?"

"Martian bloatworms," said Do-Wah. "They're very good. They taste like chicken."

Angela swallowed hard. "Um, I'll pass."

Do-Wah offered the can of slimy bloatworms to Mike.

"Don't even go there," he said.

But Cedric, sensing their commercial

value, was interested. "What's the matter? You guys wimping out? I'll try one."

Cedric took a worm out of the can, flipped it into his mouth, and swallowed. "It wasn't that bad," he said.

B.Bop looked slightly worried. "You're a brave human, Cedric," he said.

"It's no biggie. You guys eat them all the time."

"Yeah," grinned Do-Wah, "but we only eat them cooked. You've just eaten a live one!"

Cedric began to panic, coughing and trying to spit out the taste. "Am I going to die?"

B.Bop quickly put Cedric's mind at rest. "Not from a bloatworm," he said.

Cedric looked a little better. "Okay, but I think I need something to get rid of the taste. Anyone up for a quantum burger?"

The Butt-Ugly Martians looked at each other, confused by Cedric's request.

"Quantum burger? What's that?" asked B.Bop.

"Just the best chili burgers and criss-cross fries on the planet," said Angela.

"Yeah," continued Mike. "You know, fast food — burgers, chili fries, pizza... basically, if it's greasy and bad for you, it's fast food."

"Then why do you eat it?" asked 2-T.

Cedric didn't hesitate. "Because it tastes so gooood!"

Do-Wah licked his lips. "Mmmmmmmmmm. I can't wait!"

But 2-T knew better. "Forget it, Do-Wah. I know what you're thinking, but we can't go out and risk being seen."

2-T was right, but then Angela thought for a moment and an idea hit her. "Wait a minute," she said. "Maybe there is a way. It's closing time at Quantum Burgers..."

2-T caught her drift. "And if it's closed, who's gonna see us?"

Dog's ears pricked up with excitement

and Do-Wah's face lit up. "My first fast food," he said dreamily. "I could cry."

"Hold it," said B.Bop. "Aren't we forgetting something?"

"Yes," added Do-Wah, "fries with that order."

"No, someone's got to stay here to wait for Damage to send the De-Atomizer."

"Dog?" suggested 2-T hopefully.

But Dog took up a defensive stance and began to growl. 2-T reconsidered. "Okay, bad idea."

Mike had a better idea. "I'll stay," he said. "I know how to work the teleporter. Besides, I can play as much Doomrace 2000 as I want."

"Are you sure?" asked B.Bop. "That De-Atomizer is really dangerous."

But Mike was sure. "Leave it to me. I'm on it."

The lights were still on inside the fast-food joint named Quantum Burgers — a prime hangout for teenagers and the young at heart. In the window, the neon sign in the shape of a drippy, triple-chili cheeseburger still buzzed. The place was empty, however, except for one lone figure — Ronald, the counter jerk. Ronald was wiping down the counter and the tabletops, ready to close. He took special care to polish the old jukeboxes that played retro songs. He loved his job.

Ronald looked behind the counter at the cooking area. It was made up of a burger

conveyor belt, a french fry machine, and a drink dispenser. Everything was neat and shiny.

"A place for everything," Ronald said proudly, "and everything in its place." Then he headed for the door. But before he opened it, he inspected the row of star employee awards that hung on the wall. Each one had his face on it. Ronald stared at one plaque carefully. "Ugh, somebody got my award dirty," he sniveled. He wiped a finger over the award and put it to his lips. "Umm. Marshmallow. My favorite."

Continuing on his way, Ronald reached for the switches beside the front door and turned off all the lights. Then he left the building.

24

Outside, Ronald saw Angela and Cedric leaning against the burger joint's large billboard.

"Hello, beautiful night, isn't it?" the counter jerk called out as he crossed the road and headed around the corner and out of sight.

The two kids waited for Ronald to disappear. Then they gave the okay sign to the Butt-Ugly Martians who were hiding round the side of the burger joint. The coast was clear.

Meanwhile, Mike was having a whale of a time aboard Doomrace 2000.

"Man, I'm so close to the record," he enthused as he got out of the machine for a rest. "But that's gonna have to wait, because now it's time to see what's up with my favorite virtual jock."

Mike stretched and headed for 2-T's console. He pulled some levers and tuned in to video jockey Syd Severe. When he was on target, the three-dimensional head of the vj appeared above the set. The head hovered in midair, then followed Mike as the teenager walked over to the teleporter to make sure nothing had arrived from Bog yet. There was nothing there. Syd talked as Mike walked.

"That was Won Ton Yawn. And that's exactly what they're making me do... yawn. Let's see where that turkey ranks on Syd Severe's Stink-O-Meter..." Syd continued to a chorus of boos and hisses from the background, "Loser City, with the accent on loooooser!"

"Ha, you tell em, Syd." Mike laughed.

Syd went on. "And to wipe that sour sound away, I'm giving up six tickets to

Virtuopolis, the world's largest virtual amusement park and a personal 'fave' of yours truly."

"Oh, man, there's like a year's wait to get in there," said Mike.

"I'm looking for the first hoverboarder to shred down here to the station and pull off a 720° sharkwacker..."

Mike leaped up. "A 720° sharkwacker? Ha, I can do that in my sleep."

"So what are you waiting for?" yelled Syd. "You pull off the shark, I send you to the park."

Mike looked again at the teleporter. "Nothing's shown yet," he said to himself. "I can be back before anyone knows I'm gone."

He jumped on his hoverboard and made for the door. Then he stopped and took

one more look around, just to be sure. "I mean, what can happen?" he said, sounding a bit guilty. "It's not like Earth's going to come to an end. Right?" He turned and left.

Back at Quantum Burgers all was quiet. Then, one by one, heads popped up from behind the counter — first B.Bop and 2-T, then Angela and Cedric, and finally Dog, who jumped up and barked excitedly.

"It's burger time!" shouted B.Bop. "Let's eat."

"Okay," said Angela, "now remember, we can't let anyone know we've been here. Keep a low profile."

"Right," agreed Do-Wah, who was over by the light switches, "low profile." At which point, he pressed one of the switches and all the lights went on and music blared out from the sound system.

"Oh, yeah," said Angela sarcastically, "like that's keeping a low profile!"

Do-Wah winced. "Sorry!"

Back at ZAPZ, Mike had not yet returned. The arcade was completely empty, when the teleporter in the main games area suddenly came to life. Bolts of light shot from its two pincerlike arms and the middle of the machine glowed brightly. When the light disappeared, in its place stood the Molecular De-Atomizer.

Inside Quantum Burgers, Angela and Cedric sat at one of the booth tables.

"Coming here was a big mistake," said Angela, looking worried.

"What makes you say that?" asked Cedric.

Angela pointed at the counter where

fast food was flying all over the place. 2-T was feeding Dog, and Do-Wah was standing next to B.Bop, who was lying on his back beneath the burger machine.

"Pull!" shouted B.Bop.

Do-Wah pulled a lever on the burger machine and a patty of super-succulent beef fell from the dispenser and into B.Bop's mouth. B.Bop swallowed it with a

gulp, followed by a loud burp. Then he sat up and smiled contentedly. "Hit me again," he said to Do-Wah.

Angela shook her head, "I hope they don't get sick."

"Them?" said Cedric. "I'm the one who ate a live Martian bloatworm!"

As the Butt-Uglies and Dog continued to fill up with goodies, something far more stomach churning was happening at ZAPZ.

Near the amusement arcade stood Gorgon, holding a tracking device. Its blinking light indicated a strong signal from the ZAPZ arcade building. Gorgon looked up at the dilapidated ZAPZ sign, then laughed wickedly to himself as he headed for the boarded-up entrance.

Once inside, he spotted the teleporter.

His nasty smile reappeared as he spotted exactly what he was looking for — the Molecular De-Atomizer.

"There you are, my destructive little

friend," he said with evil relish, reaching into the teleporter and grabbing his prize.

Meanwhile, the Butt-Ugly Martians and Dog were sprawled out on the floor of Quantum Burgers, groaning. Angela and Cedric stood over them.

"Guys, come on... aren't you done yet?" Angela asked impatiently.

Her question was greeted with a loud "BUUURRRP!"

"They're done," said Cedric.

The Butt-Uglies hauled themselves up and followed Angela and Cedric out into the night.

Before long, they had reached the safety of ZAPZ. 2-T headed straight for the teleporter. "That's strange," he said. "According to this machine, the De-Atomizer has arrived."

"Then, uh... where is it?" asked Do-Wah.

"And where's Mike?" Angela added.

"I hope he's not messing with the De-Atomizer," said B.Bop, looking worried.

"Yeah," said Do-Wah, "one wrong move and we'll be Grekian toast..."

Do-Wah was just about to say something else, when the door to ZAPZ opened and in walked Mike. He waved the free passes to Virtuopolis above his head.

"Hey guys," he yelled, "great news! I won us free passes to Virtuopolis."

The Butt-Ugly Martians looked at him. They did not look happy.

"What's wrong?" asked Mike.

B.Bop looked at Mike. "Mike, tell us you've got the De-Atomizer."

"Because if you don't," interrupted Angela, "somebody stole it."

"Stole it?" said Mike. "I was only gone a little while...oh, man!"

At that point, Dog began sniffing. The Butt-Uglies followed suit.

"Wait a second," said Do-Wah. "Do you smell something?"

Cedric made a face. "Well, you guys did polish off a cow and a half — with the works."

2-T put his nose to the floor and sniffed loudly. Suddenly, he lifted his head. "It's

Gorgon," he said with a hint of disgust in his voice. "He was here."

B.Bop began to talk quickly to the other two Butt-Uglies in Martian. He finished with three ominous human words: "Say bye bye!"

"That didn't sound good," said Mike as the Martians threw one another decidedly worried looks.

MIKE'S IN TROUBLE

"ALL RIGHT, YOU'VE got our attention," said Mike. "Who, or what, is Gorgon?"

"He's from a smelly, underachieving, alien race of fire-spitting, weapon-thieving shape-shifters," replied B.Bop.

"Sounds like my math teacher," said Angela sarcastically.

Cedric looked up. "So I take it this Gorgon guy is pretty dangerous, huh?"

"Oh, you could say that...and now he's got the Molecular De-Atomizer, just to make things a little bit worse," said B.Bop, getting more and more worried.

Mike was feeling awful. "Well, then let's just find him and get it back," he said.

"It's not that easy, Mike," said Do-Wah. "A shape-shifter could be anywhere. He could be anyone. He could be me..."

Mike looked at Do-Wah, confused.

"Well, maybe not me — I'm me. He could be Angela," said Do-Wah, getting a bit out of his depth.

Everyone looked in Angela's direction.

"Don't look at me. I don't smell and I got four A's last semester."

Mike didn't know what to do. He felt completely responsible. How could he have left ZAPZ unattended? "This is all my fault," he said desperately, holding his head in his hands.

Meanwhile, Gorgon stood outside a hangar at the old military airfield he was using as his hideout. He looked carefully at the Molecular De-Atomizer in his hand. On its surface he saw buttons and Martian symbols. Gorgon studied the symbols. "Blast! These instructions are in Martian," he cried. But he wasn't going to let a small setback get in his way. "I don't need instructions!" he said defiantly.

Then Gorgon raised the De-Atomizer and aimed it at one of the abandoned airplanes parked on the airfield. He fiddled with the buttons, but nothing happened. All he got was a series of buzzes and bleeps. Angered by his failure to fire

the thing, Gorgon pushed furiously at the buttons. But still nothing happened — except more whirrs and buzzes. The big green alien was frustrated. He breathed deeply and his eyes burned red as he spat a fireball at the airplane. There was a blinding explosion and all that was left of the plane was a smoking black hulk.

But this destruction didn't make Gorgon feel any better. He looked at the De-Atomizer and roared, "I need someone to show me how this thing works!"

Back at ZAPZ arcade, 2-T frantically pressed switches on his console as he tried to pick up Gorgon on his monitor, while B.Bop and Do-Wah paced anxiously.

"2-T, do you think you can find this Gorgon guy?" asked Cedric.

"He'd better," said B.Bop, "or we'll all be saying good-bye to this planet."

Mike groaned, "Oh, you guys, I feel awful. This is all my fault."

B.Bop tried to reassure him. "Nothing you can do about it now. So take it easy."

2-T was getting nowhere. "Oh, it's no use. My equipment's just not strong enough to locate his life force. I could make something, but we don't have that kind of time."

"Wait a minute," said B.Bop. "Are you thinking what I'm thinking?"

"Yes! No. What?" replied 2-T, confused.

"That alien hunter, Muldoon!" cried B.Bop. "He's got an alien detector."

"Exactly," said Do-Wah as the others looked at him in disbelief. "What? I know a good idea when I hear one."

But Mike wasn't sure. "Wait a minute. Muldoon's not going to just let us walk in and use his stuff."

"Oh, I think he's going to be a little too busy to notice," said B.Bop.

A little later, the kids arrived on their hoverboards outside Stoat Muldoon's missile silo headquarters. The place was bristling with all kinds of anti-alien devices. Muldoon was dozing in front of his console. "Okay, Mr. President," he said sleepily, "I'll save the planet...just please, stop your begging..."

Suddenly, the lights on Muldoon's console panel flashed madly and a siren wailed. The alien hunter was rudely awakened. "What the... Mother McCreedy!" he gasped, switching on his monitor screen to see Do-Wah, B.Bop, and Dog zooming around outside. "Aliens! A pod of them! They're all over the place!"

He got out of his hoverchair and raced for the door. But in his rush to get out, he left his alien tracking device on top of his console.

At the base of the silo, Stoat Muldoon boarded his hovervan and fired it up. Flames spewed out of the wheels as the hovervan rose up and made its way deftly between the two steel doors that secured the roof of the silo tube.

"Here he comes," called Do-Wah.

As Muldoon guided the hovervan out into the desert, his eyes focused on Do-Wah

and B.Bop aboard their OMABs, and Dog hovering nearby. The Butt-Uglies waved when they saw Muldoon.

"Over here, Mr. Muldoon," called B.Bop, wickedly taunting the alien hunter.

"He knows who I am," said Stoat Muldoon proudly. "My reputation precedes me."

"Come and get us, stoatmuldoon.com!" shouted Do-Wah defiantly.

Muldoon was impressed. "Why, they've even got my website address. These aliens have done their homework, all right, but are they prepared for this?"

Muldoon quickly pressed a button that fired a tractor beam from his hovervan. It headed straight for Do-Wah, B.Bop, and Dog, but they were too fast for it. The beam sped past them and crashed into some rocks, as the Butt-Uglies and Dog turned and swooped away.

As Muldoon tried to figure out what to do next, Mike, on his hoverboard, and 2-T, aboard his OMAB, went through the steel doors and glided down the long missile silo tube into Muldoon's control center. Angela and Cedric stood guard outside.

Meanwhile, Muldoon continued his pursuit of Do-Wah, B.Bop, and Dog. He wasn't having much luck.

"It's going to take the skills of a double-jointed acrobat to pull in these alien rascals...oh, but they're going to learn! You don't mess with Muldoon," said the alien hunter as he veered off in pursuit of the pesky aliens.

But, just as he thought his luck had changed, the Butt-Uglies and Dog disappeared into a cloud. "Ah, the old 'hide behind the cloud' trick," said Muldoon gleefully. "Alien, I was doing that one long before you were born. Hiyeeeee!" With that, Muldoon followed the three aliens into the cloud.

However, once they had lured Muldoon into the cloud, Do-Wah and B.Bop headed off, leaving Dog to lead the alien hunter on a wild goose chase. Dog tapped on the hovervan, then zoomed off into the distance with Muldoon following.

Once inside Muldoon's hq, Mike and 2-T began to look around.

"Wow!" said Mike, eyeing the equipment. "Look at this stuff. It's scary."

2-T had already spotted Muldoon's alien tracking device, or MATD. "Okay, this is it," he said. "This is what we need."

"Can you work it?" asked Mike urgently.

"I'll try," said 2-T as he pressed a button on the MATD. Its screen lit up and showed a small dot.

"Is that Gorgon?" asked Mike excitedly.

"No, that's me," said 2-T, pressing more buttons on the MATD. "Hold on."

Mike watched as another image formed on the screen, and a new dot appeared.

"If I'm right, that's Gorgon," said 2-T. "He seems to be at some sort of airfield..."

"I know that place," said Mike.

2-T began to program the MATD. "I'll just lock in the coordinates...and..." But before he had time to finish what he was saying, his voice faltered. Mike was gone! He was on his hoverboard and flying through the great steel doors of the silo..."Mike!" 2-T cried.

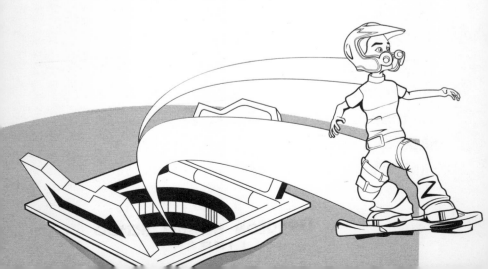

B.Bop and Do-Wah had returned to the entrance of the missile silo to join 2-T and the kids.

"What did you do with Stoat Muldoon?" asked Cedric.

"He's on a wild Dog chase," chuckled B.Bop. "Where's Mike?"

"We think he went after the device alone," said Angela, sounding worried. "He was feeling so guilty and everything."

"We've gotta get to him before Gorgon does," said Do-Wah.

"Follow me," ordered 2-T.

The Butt-Uglies and Angela and Cedric wasted no time. They headed off as fast as they could, following 2-T. Their only hope was that 2-T knew where they could find Mike.

Thankfully, 2-T got the old airfield's location dead right. As they neared the site, B.Bop turned on his wrist gauntlet communicator. "Mike! Come in, Mike!" he called urgently. "Mike, do you copy?"

"Yeah, I read you," said Mike.

"We're coming. Wait for us," said B.Bop.

But Mike wasn't prepared to wait. "I can't. If it wasn't for me... Well, I'm going to fix all that right now. I'm going in..."

"Mike, wait!" Angela pleaded. "It's not your fault. There's no way you could have stopped Gorgon. Please, just wait for help."

Mike, however, was determined. "Thanks,

Angela," he said, "but I've gotta do this alone. Mike out."

At the old airfield, Gorgon was inside his hangar, still trying to get the De-Atomizer to work. Mike was watching him from a hatch in the hangar's roof. "I just need to distract him. But how?" he said to himself. Just then, he noticed a large bolt nearby. It gave him an idea.

Gorgon was getting more and more angry with the De-Atomizer. "Haven't these Martians ever heard of a simple on/off switch?" he fumed.

Mike kept an eye on the alien, then threw the bolt into the hangar. It landed with a crack. Startled, Gorgon dropped the De-Atomizer and turned, while Mike hoverboarded in and grabbed the device.

"Got it!" he said triumphantly. Then, as he flew off, Mike yelled to Gorgon, "So long, sucker!"

"We'll see about that," replied Gorgon menacingly, as he grabbed his energy light bola, and aimed it at Mike. The weapon began to emit powerful red-yellow rays. The rays quickly engulfed the boy and hauled him into the evil alien's hangar!

Mike landed facedown. He looked up at Gorgon with an embarrassed smile on his face. "Uh...hi th-th-there," he stuttered. "Um...Welcome to Earth, Mr. Gorgon...yuk! What smells?"

Outside, Angela, Cedric, and the three Butt-Ugly Martians had finally arrived at the hangar. They rushed to the open door

and looked in. They were greeted by the sight of Mike at the end of the building, held in an energy rope.

No-one else seemed to be there, so the Butt-Uglies ran in to free their friend. Angela and Cedric hung back at the hangar door to keep watch.

"Are you okay?" asked B.Bop.

"Yeah," he replied. "Boy, am I glad to see you guys."

The Butt-Uglies quickly untied Mike, who backed away from them a few paces. Then, to their horror, Mike began to change. His body started to emit a blinding light, and in seconds, he reformed as the terrible shape-shifter, Gorgon!

The alien fired his energy light bola, releasing an energy bolt at the Butt-Ugly Martians. It whizzed through the air and wrapped around all three, instantly pinning them to the ground.

"Welcome, Martians," said Gorgon smiling. "If I'm not mistaken, I believe you came for this."

The gloating alien pointed to a cage

hanging above his head, where Mike was imprisoned. The bars were created from lasers, making escape impossible.

"Mike!" yelled Do-Wah.

"Let him go, Gorgon," said B.Bop.

But the evil alien took no notice, and there was nothing the Butt-Ugly Martians could do to help their Earthling friend.

Outside the hangar, Angela and Cedric had seen everything. "We've got to do something," whispered Angela.

Cedric nodded agreement. "I've got an idea. Follow me." Silently, they mounted their hoverboards and sped off across the desert.

Meanwhile, Gorgon had begun to pace around his captives. Mike was completely helpless, and although the Martians struggled as hard as they could, they could not break free from the powerful energy force pinning them to the ground. The situation was bleak.

"You Martians are so easily beaten," said Gorgon, grinning wickedly at his prisoners.

2-T looked at him. "Come on, Gorgon, The boy can't hurt you. Let him go."

Gorgon thought for a moment about 2-T's request. "After you show me how this works," he said, holding up the Molecular De-Atomizer and pointing to the Martian symbols on the device.

"No dice," said B.Bop firmly.

In the desert nearby, Cedric had put his idea to work. He now rode aboard an Exo-Bot, the huge mechanical fighting machine created by Tech Commando 2-T.

The Exo-Bot had a communicator that allowed Cedric to talk to Angela. She was at the controls of a second Exo-Bot. The problem was that neither of them had any idea how to operate the giant armored machines.

"How do you work this thing?" yelled Cedric, extremely frustrated.

"Search me," said Angela. "But I've seen Mike do this."

Angela pulled a lever on the control console and the Exo-Bot jerked forward. Cedric did the same and for a few seconds the two Exo-Bots lurched awkwardly across the desert. Angela and Cedric's hands worked feverishly at the controls. Finally, the Exo-Bots ran straight into each other, and fell backward into the sand.

"Um. This may take a while," said Cedric dryly.

"I'm afraid we don't have a while," Angela snapped back.

Inside Gorgon's aircraft hangar, the Butt-Ugly Martians were still refusing to tell the alien how to work the De-Atomizer. "My patience is wearing thin," said Gorgon menacingly.

"You know we can't tell you how it works," said B.Bop. "With it you'll destroy Earth and any other planet that gets in your way."

"You'll rule the universe," added 2-T.

Exasperated, Gorgon touched his wrist gauntlet and aimed it at Mike. "Then you leave me no choice," he sneered. "Say good-bye to your friend."

TIME FOR BASEBALL PRACTICE!

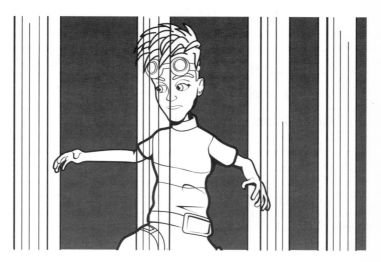

GORGON LOOKED DOWN at the Butt-Ugly Martians and licked his lips in anticipation. "Your little friend is running out of time," he said.

Meanwhile, Mike was thinking as fast as he could. Suddenly he had an idea. Making sure that Gorgon had his back to him, he winked at B.Bop, 2-T, and Do-Wah. The three Butt-Uglies stopped struggling to get free and stared up at Mike, confused.

"I think Mike's trying to tell us something," whispered B.Bop.

"That, or he's got something in his eye," Do-Wah whispered back.

Mike began to put on an act. "I don't want to die," he said dramatically. "I want to live. Please, Gorgon. I can help you."

"And how can you do that?" thundered Gorgon impatiently.

Mike was improvising madly. "I...I can read Martian," he said. "I took it in summer school."

Gorgon's eyebrows arched upward. He was interested.

Mike continued, "I'll translate the instructions, but only if you free me."

The Butt-Ugly Martians had caught on

to Mike's scam and were ready to play their part.

"Don't do it, Mike," called out B.Bop. "Think of your friends."

"Think of your family," said 2-T.

"Think of your planet," added Do-Wah.

But Mike ignored their pleas. "What do you say, Gorgon?"

The alien considered for a moment, then released Mike and handed him the Molecular De-Atomizer. "Don't try anything stupid," he said. "I still have your Martian friends."

But before Mike could do anything more, Cedric and Angela came in through the hangar doors, aboard the Exo-Bots.

"Over here, stinky!" shouted Angela.

"It's Cedric and Angela," cried B.Bop.

"Who taught them to drive Exo-Bots?" asked Do-Wah.

"Who cares?" yelled 2-T. "Just go get Gorgon, you guys!"

But Gorgon was not phased by the Exo-Bots. "Looks like we've got company," he said casually.

Cedric quickly began working levers and

talking into his communicator. "Time to put this alien in a time warp," he said fiercely.

Angela looked across to Cedric and yelled, "Let's do it!"

The two Exo-Bots rushed into the hangar, swinging their long arms and heading for Gorgon. But the reptilelike alien showed no fear at all. He glared at the machines and took a deep breath. Then, as his eyes turned blood red, he spat out two flaming fireballs.

The fireballs flew through the air like cannon shot, and hit each of the Exo-Bots, sending them crashing against the hangar wall. Cedric and Angela only just managed to retain control of their battered machines.

"This guy's hot stuff," Cedric said.

Angela was having problems. "Tell that to my Exo-Bot," she said. "It can't take much more of this."

Cedric pondered for a moment. Then he said, "I feel like a game of baseball."

"What?" yelled Angela.

"Just follow me," replied Cedric.

Gorgon turned to spit more fireballs at the Exo-Bots. However, this time, Cedric and Angela were ready. The kids used the arms of their Exo-Bots as giant baseball bats. They swung for all they were worth and hit the fireballs back at Gorgon! But instead of hitting the alien, the fireballs whizzed past him and hit the energy light bola holding the three Butt-Uglies, causing it to explode and disappear. The Martians were free!

"Great shot, guys!" yelled B.Bop.

Gorgon screamed with fury and spat three fireballs at the Butt-Uglies. But the Martians were too quick for him and easily jumped out of the way.

The alien then turned his attention on Mike and aimed a fireball at him. Mike was not so quick, but luckily Do-Wah was there to rescue him. He jumped across and pushed Mike out of the way, saving him from instant incineration! Mike thudded to the ground and the Molecular De-Atomizer flew out of his hands.

It was time for the Butt-Uglies to do something extreme. B.Bop looked at his two companions and they nodded. "It's time for... BKM!" he said.

The moment the Butt-Ugly Martians transformed into BKM, they became super Martians, equipped with the coolest weapons and tech outfits in the galaxy!

When all three had transformed, they thumped to the ground and yelled their battle cry, "LET'S GET UGLY!"

Then like lightning they picked up Mike, along with Cedric and Angela in their Exo-Bots, and flew them out of the hangar to safety.

Spitting fireballs, Gorgon chased them. All he could do was watch as the fireballs bounced harmlessly off the Butt-Uglies' BKM suits.

But Gorgon could defend himself, too. As the Butt-Uglies flew above him, the alien took another light bola and swung it in front of him, creating a shield of light. When the Butt-Uglies fired powerful photon rays at him, the shield deflected the rays.

Do-Wah looked on. "Darn, he's good!" said the Martian, impressed.

Luckily, B.Bop had a plan. "Do-Wah, go and get the De-Atomizer," he said quickly. "2-T and I will keep Gorgon busy."

Cedric and Angela were now out of their Exo-Bots and were standing with Mike on a wing of one of the old airplanes. They were watching the Butt-Uglies in awe.

As Do-Wah sped back into the hangar to find the De-Atomizer, 2-T and B.Bop got to work on Gorgon. B.Bop soared overhead as Gorgon defended himself against 2-T's photon rays. Then B.Bop began to fly around in a circle, directly above Gorgon. He flew faster and faster, and before Gorgon knew what was happening, he was caught inside a mini-tornado. Dust and sand blew everywhere, confusing the rattled alien.

Gorgon still spat out fireballs, but they were flying out of control in all directions. Suddenly, a few headed for the kids, forcing them to duck down fast. Luckily, the balls screeched past them.

Do-Wah appeared with the Molecular

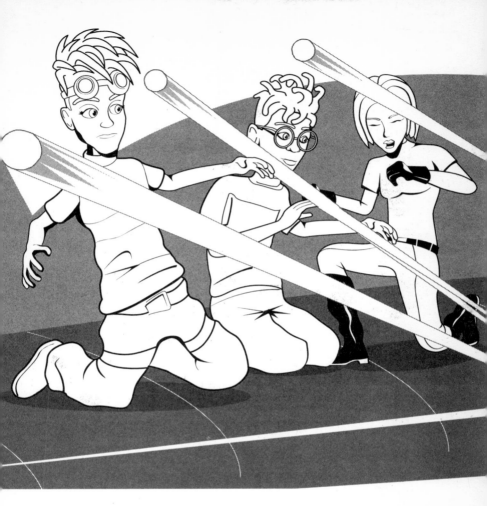

De-Atomizer. He pressed a few buttons and fired straight at Gorgon. "It's time to say, 'Hasta la vista, baby!'" Do-Wah shouted triumphantly.

Do-Wah and the others watched as Gorgon was engulfed by the Molecular De-Atomizer's orange-red bubble. There was nothing he could do, and in no time at all, he fizzled, crackled, popped, and disappeared!

"Yes!" yelled the Butt-Ugly Martians in unison. "Who da Martians?" they cried, congratulating one another as they went into a well deserved victory dance.

"We da Martians," cried Do-Wah.

Mike, Angela, and Cedric jumped up and down and cheered as they watched the Martians celebrate. They felt safe, until they heard a strange noise coming from the sky above. But soon they were laughing, as they recognized a familiar voice singing, "I dream of Jeannie with the light brown hair..."

Seconds later, they saw Dog fly out of the puffy white clouds, and behind him,

still in hot pursuit, came Stoat Muldoon in his hovervan!

Stoat was exhausted but determined. "Hold yourself together Muldoon," he said. "Keep going and THINK! You need that Dog to prove that aliens really do exist. There's got to be some way to trap the robo pooch...Wait, hey, I've got it! Why didn't I think of it earlier? It's brilliant." Then he called sweetly, "Here doggie, doggie, doggie...Come to Papa!"

"Good grief!" exclaimed Cedric. The kids and the Butt-Uglies laughed, as the alien hunter flew off, chasing Dog into the distance once more.

Later that day, at Quantum Burgers, Ronald was busy wiping down the counter in front of him. Mike, Angela, and Cedric stood nearby, discussing their latest amazing adventure. Now that they were friends with the Butt-Ugly Martians, life was never boring. Ronald, the counter nerd, was listening carefully to their conversation.

"I wonder if other kids have ever had to risk their lives to save the planet from evil aliens?" Mike asked Angela and Cedric.

Cedric was thinking of Gorgon. "You think we got him?"

"He's history!" replied Mike. "I don't think we'll be seeing Gorgon again."

Angela was not so sure. "But how do you know?" she said. "He's an alien shape-shifter, remember?"

Suddenly, the kids noticed that Ronald was watching them and hanging on their every word. They decided to have some fun at the expense of the counter jerk.

"Oh, yeah, he could be anybody," said Mike. Then he turned abruptly and pointed

straight at Ronald. "Even you!" he said menacingly to the confused Quantum Burgers' employee.

Ronald looked up in surprise, "What? What did I do?"

Angela walked over to Ronald and stared at him strangely. "By day, employee of the month. By night...a fire-breathing alien!" she said excitedly, frightening poor Ronald out of his skin.

"Ahhhhhh!" cried the unfortunate counter jerk as his face went even whiter than normal.

"Relax," said Cedric, smiling. "We're just kidding."

Ronald grinned uncomfortably. "Oh, yeah, I get it. That's funny. Ha, ha, ha...Evil alien...Okay, I'll go 'fire up' your order. Ha, ha, ha..." Ronald laughed again. Then, as he slowly turned away from the kids, his eyes glowed fiery red and his laugh turned into an diabolical roar...

DON'T MISS ANY OF THE EXCITING BUTT-UGLY ADVENTURES:

BUTT-UGLY MARTIANS #1
THE BIG BANG THEORY

Alien Hunter Stoat Muldoon has captured Dog and taken him to a top-secret government laboratory. There the terrifying, laser-cutting scientist, Dr. Brady Hacksaw is planning to take Dog apart! Now the Butt-Uglies and the kids are on a highly hazardous rescue mission.

Things only get worse when the kids encounter a Nitchup, a seemingly harmless alien who will explode if exposed to Earth's atmosphere—too bad no one thought to tell Cedric that before he freed the little guy. Can the Butt-Uglies save the day?

Join the adventure and help the Martians save Earth! LET'S GET UGLY!

AND COMING SOON . . .

BUTT-UGLY MARTIANS #3
THAT'S NO PUDDLE, THAT'S ANGELA

2-T has invented a new device that will let the Martians go out in public by making them invisible. The only problem is that if the device is used on humans it turns them into puddles of goo—and Mike just used it on Angela!

Now Mike and Cedric have to find the Butt-Uglies to get their help changing Angela back. But the Butt-Uglies are off investigating a series of mysterious earthquakes in the middle of the desert. Can they find out who's behind the tremors or will the ground continue to shake, rattle 'n' roll?